good deed rain

54 Books by Allen Frost

...Ohio Trio...Bowl of Water...Another Life...
...Home Recordings...The Mermaid Translation...
...The Selected Correspondence of Kenneth
Patchen...The Wonderful Stupid Man...
...Saint Lemonade...Playground...Roosevelt...
...5 Novels...The Sylvan Moore Show...
...Town in a Cloud...A Flutter of Birds Passing
Through Heaven: A Tribute to Robert Sund...
..At the Edge of America..Lake Erie Submarine..
...The Book of Ticks...I Can Only Imagine...
...The Orphanage of Abandoned Teenagers...
..Different Planet..Go With the Flow: A Tribute
to Clyde Sanborn...Homeless Sutra...
..The Lake Walker..A Hundred Dreams Ago..
..Almost Animals..The Robotic Age..Kennedy..
...Fable...Elbows & Knees: Essays and Plays...
...The Last Paper Stars...Walt Amherst is Awake...
....When You Smile You Let in Light....
...Pinocchio in America...Florida...
..Blue Anthem Wailing..The Welfare Office..
...Island Air...Imaginary Someone...
....Violet of the Silent Movies....
...The Tin Can Telephone...Heaven Crayon...
..Old Salt..A Field of Cabbages..River Road..
...The Puttering Marvel...Something Bright...
...The Trillium Witch...Cosmonaut...
...Thriftstore Madonna...Half a Giraffe...
..Lexington Brown & The Pond Projector..
.....The Robert Huck Museum.....
...Mrs. Magnusson & Friends...
...Magic Island...

Magic
Island

MAGIC ISLAND © 2022
Allen Frost, Good Deed Rain
Bellingham, Washington
ISBN: 978-1-0880-4379-0

Writing: Allen Frost
Illustrations: Allen Frost
Cover painting: "Shifting Terrain" by Laura Vasyutynska
Back cover photograph: "Walker Art Building, Southwest View," Call#2968, Courtesy of the George J. Mitchell Department of Special Collections & Archives, Bowdoin College Library, Brunswick, Maine.
Photo scrap on page 80 believed to be from *The Bowdoin Orient*.
Cover Production: Katrina Svoboda
Quotes:
Options, Robert Sheckley, Pyramid Books, New York, 1975.
The Life and Zen Haiku Poetry of Santoka Taneda, Sumita Okama, Tuttle Publishing, 2021.
Apple: TFK!

We float here and there on currents of what we want and what we don't want, what we desire and what desires us.

—Robert Sheckley

I wandered aimlessly for a long time. And it was not only my body that was wandering aimlessly, but my mind was wandering too. I felt bitter about what should have been, and was afflicted by those things that would not go away. But then, finally I was able to settle down with the "things that are." And it was there that I discovered myself.

—Santoka Taneda

MAGIC ISLAND

Allen Frost

Good Deed Rain ◊ Bellingham, Washington ◊ 2022

We're surrounded by brick temples, palm trees, tropical flowers. Here we are in California, my son and I, and I'm writing these words to go with *Magic Island*. I have tried to create a companion for him as he goes to college, by writing a book about time travel.

There's a machine in this book that will allow you to see what happened when Gypsum Tweed was my son's age. At least it shows certain memories—hopefully memories that have some meaning. Anyway, with this book we are able to go back to moments that stand out and might even serve as lessons.

Not that I'm one to give advice, our hero in this book makes his share of mistakes. There's not much more I can really do but say where I've been and what I remember and hope that it helps to hold onto what ought to be precious.

Warm sunshine, blue sky, petals, everywhere the air is like some Egyptian spice.

And now I'm back in Washington where it's 40 degrees and people are dressed for winter. What happened to California? It's still there, I'm the one who has moved on. Back to where I find myself at work. For my lunchbreak I put on my jacket and walk up the woods behind my office. At the hilltop I hear an owl. I stop and look for it. It called from a hidden place in the trees and then I saw a flash of speckled wings as it flew.

—AF, in May of 2022

starring

33.   attraction
34.   halls and shadows
35.   blurred
36.   discontent
37.   mistakes
38.   view of the trees
39.   celebrity
40.   reason
41.   sound effects
42.   haunted
43.   the otherworld
44.   rumor
45.   the collected essays
46.   not a word
47.   publication
48.   filled with hours
49.   cotton
50.   the piano
51.   celestial
52.   hypnosis
53.   magic
54.   music
55.   other radios
56.   unexpected
57.   the back row
58.   greetings
59.   legacy
60.   zen
61.   rabbits
62.   philosophy
63.   real life
64.   joy and adventure
65.   successful
66.   ideas
67.   inspiration
68.   melting
69.   style

70.   girls
71.   together
72.   happy
73.   so long
74.   2:22
75.   the moonflowers
76.   job posting
77.   submissions
78.   the printshop
79.   the stars
80.   momentum
81.   another wall
82.   reading
83.   destined
84.   easy
85.   experience
86.   computers
87.   luck
88.   advice
89.   lifted
90.   summertime
91.   dandelions
92.   ending
93.   time
94.   agatha
95.   memories
96.   signing off

MOXIE

1. *the story*

This is the story of a fool. He didn't last long, only four years, and when school was over, he was gone. This book is a journey back in time to then. There is little to guide us there—a few scraps—mostly it is whatever swirls in this faulty memory machine.

2. *arrivals*

The story begins with Jim McBrady. That was the old pickup truck loaded with Gypsum Tweed's duffel bag and boxes. His grandfather drove him, a Salem cigarette in the corner of his mouth.

The fact that they resembled the start of *Sanford & Son* never occurred to Gypsum. The old green truck reminded him of summers going with his grandfather to the boatyard. They would meet Gene there, he would appear beside an overturned hull planted with blue flowers. Gypsum loved to listen to the two of them shoot the breeze. While they drove home, Gypsum would hang his arm out the window. He would tap the hot metal door where the letters spelled out

JIM MCBRADY
CONSTRUCTION

in yellow letters outlined with rust.

Gypsum's grandfather drove him to the bridge and they crossed to Magic Island. There was a lot of traffic, College Street was crowded with parents and new arrivals. Bags and boxes and suitcases were stacked all over the cars. Jim McBrady fit right in.

3. *around*

Gypsum was a long way from the rest of his family on the other side of America, but he had his grandparents and relatives who lived around Magic Island. Anytime he got lonely he could take a gondola off campus and visit. One grandmother lived on Thompson Street, in the brown wooden house where his father grew up. His other grandparents lived in a cove on a pine-covered hill. The Navy balloons would buzz overhead, and Gypsum would go running outside to see them.

4. *the memory machine*

Perhaps it was wrong of me to describe this assignment as "a rollicking, rousing, heartwarming romance, a taut tour-de-force of the human psyche." Was that too much? It was a hard sell, but it did gather me a crew of fairly competent workers who have proven worthy at sifting through the dust of time to reassemble a story that was good as lost. Were they expecting Gypsum Tweed to be a young Marlon Brando, or John Keats? Who am I to dissuade them? Write what you notice, I tell them. The memory machine is rumbling. They are huddled around it, taking notes, handing them over to typists who give the finished pages to a temp who runs them to me. My job is simple, I'm just the narrator.

5. *potions*

Jekyll Hall is a four-story brick dorm and home for Gypsum's freshman year. He shared a crowded room on the first floor with two other boys. Louie, from Atlantic City and the other is named Beta-Hy, from Mars. Gypsum never met a Martian before. It went okay for a while, but then after a while it didn't. There was that little wooden box of Martian potions. Gypsum wondered if he had been poisoned. Gypsum felt and acted in ways he never knew he could. Who knows why? He should have gone to Magic Island expecting it to be like one of those adventures he read about. The entire wall of his room back home was shelved with *National Geographics* from the 1930s to the 1960s. Why couldn't he be an intrepid explorer too? He was still in a cocoon, and breaking free of it wouldn't be easy. That's part of what we're watching. Already I can tell this will be a problem with our project. Looking back, watching it unfold, unable to break the spell he is in. Some people have a lot to learn. There were things Gypsum never contemplated until he took "Karma 101."

6. *the union*

The bookstore was in the basement of the Student Union. Gypsum had his class schedule and stood in a long line that slowed down the stairs into the cramped room. The space was stacked to the ceiling with books, making arches to walk under. It was a miracle they didn't rain down on everyone as the students jostled and reached for what they needed. A girl asked if Gypsum could get her math textbook, up high on the shelf. He did and he told her good luck with that class and she laughed. Gypsum had his blue checkbook in his coat pocket and the stack of books he carried to the cashier would be the first page. The Union was also home to a cafeteria and the mailroom. He would return to them later. As he came back outside, he looked above to the third floor. Surrounded by ivy and bricks, he heard the radio station playing music out the open window.

7. *a great author*

Gypsum Tweed was determined to be a great author. He didn't know how that was supposed to happen, except that maybe it began with reading, reading, reading. He was part of a long flowing river, and he would start at the beginning with *The Odyssey* and row his way through Medieval Europe and Shakespeare and finally sail to America. His pockets would be full of scribbled notes and he would be ready for his own books to find him.

8. *alone*

That first week was strange as a different planet. Magic Island was the first time he was alone like this and finding himself that way, even if his life was all laid out with classes, instructions, assignments, deadlines, it was up to him, he was on his own. At night the room was haunted by the sound of snoring. The tall pale walls and ceiling, the radiator hissing. For the first time, Gypsum was by himself, marooned in a room with a Martian.

9. *homesick*

He met a student from Sikkim. There's a land Gypsum knew! He read about it in a 1963 *National Geographic.* The state animal is the red panda. Who else could he share that knowledge with? Gypsum knew that kid was homesick. They met a few times at the dining hall near Colds Tower. They talked about the royal family of Sikkim. Gypsum's reference was twenty years out of date. He didn't know the prince had already become a king.

10. *new people*

There were so many new people. Everyone was there from all over. A girl from Jupiter and her roommate from the moon lived across the hall. How strange that students were attracted to this place in time. The island was linked to land by gondolas on wires, and a stone bridge for cars, and when the tide went out you could even take your chances and cross the flats to the other shore. Otherwise, students were in their own world. You could meet someone and become friends. It's mysterious how that happens, magnetic intersecting fields or some other power beyond our knowing. Magic Island has been doing it for a long time.

11. *hello*

The first thing he noticed about Sacco was his books. Gypsum followed Louie to Hawkins Hall. Louie knew someone in a dorm room there. While they were talking, Gypsum drifted around. Sacco wasn't there at the time, but Gypsum was drawn to the bookshelf. All the Vonnegut books were there and others he never heard of. Believe it or not, it would take until another winter before they met, later on, when Gypsum was at a friend's house. Not far away, the bridge was lit for night with blue lanterns. Before he saw Sacco, Gypsum heard his African guitar. There was a big Tom Waits poster on his door as Gypsum pushed it open to finally say hello.

Your Bowdoin College address is:

Allen W. Frost

M. U. Box 311
Bowdoin College
Brunswick, Maine   04011

Your Box Combination is:

Right three turns to   GH
Left to the second   CD
Right to   F
Turn latch key left

12. *311*

At some point after lunch, Gypsum would get his mail. In the basement of the Union, just off the cafeteria, was a narrow hall. One wall was lined from floor to ceiling with little gold doors, each one with its own numbered window. He could look in 311 and see if anything was there. Sometimes he got letters from a girl in Oregon. What did he know about holding on to someone three thousand miles away? He sent her handmade postcard collages. Funny letters with drawings. What did he know? On a date, he took her to see *Stranger Than Paradise.*

13. *serenade*

Here's what an oddball Gypsum was. He serenaded a girl on the 6th floor of Applefield Hall. Of all things, he recited a Petrarch poem while Moose played a Willie Nelson riff on a guitar. It was a crazy thing to do, wouldn't you say? But that's the way he was—he lived life like a movie. Nobody opened her door and he and Moose ran off down the loud metal stairs. A real smooth operation. Back in his room, Gypsum survived the heartbreak by typing a play about it. As his poetic narrator explained in the spotlight, "Naturally, as writer of the play, it is my duty to give this tragedy a happy ending, but this is, after all, reality. And life requires a great deal of suffering."

                                        ADVICE FROM CICERO
                                           Allen Frost

     The scene is a dark stage at the moment with a spotlight revealing
a figure who will soon speak. He is wearing casual attire but due to
his predominant position decided to wear a tie with his light blue
shirt. Now that it is quiet, he speaks.

Narrator: This is not a play of imaginings from some idiot's head,
          but instead, a sonnet of actual love, unfancified and not
          idealized by the pen of mighty authors. Indeed, my play
          doesn't make use of dramatic balconies or tear-filled
          tombs; but instead focuses on the talk in a dorm room and
          an unplayed guitar. But let my play speak for itself; as
          my past becomes your present.

The lights now go on, exposing a dorm room. As a college provided
room, it is expectedly shabby. It is furnished with two chairs which
stand apart from each other and face one another. There is also a
couch. The chairs and couch are arranged only a small distance from
each other. A wall occupies the background. There is a window on the
wall with a third chair against its pane. This chair is sometimes
used as a lookout. A guitar in its stand is not far from the window.
In the two chairs and couch are seated Alexander, Cicero and Frank in
various states of reading the newspaper. Each person has a different
section. Cicero as a practical character is reading the front page.
Alexander, being a dreamer-romantic reads the comic pages and Frank
reads the sports page. Alexander, stretched on the floor, head resting
on a chair while he reads, addresses Cicero.

Alexander: Why is it Spider Man and Mike Nomad are both falling in
           love in the same week I am? It's a worldwide conspiracy.

Frank (Intent on the statistics in the Sports Page): Hey, the girls
           ninth grade Ping Pong team from my home town has advanced
           to the finals!

Alexander: Frank, Spiderman and I are suffering the conflict of our

                                                                      I

14. *stardust*

Moose lived at the north end of Jekyll Hall. He loved that *Stardust* album. Every day he would play along to it and Gypsum would sit and listen. Whatever happened to Moose? He wanted to find a girl in school and get married the same way his parents did, and he wanted that life that worked for them, to live in a house in a neighborhood with a station wagon and kids tumbling around. That was another sort of movie. They were everywhere, like birds. All you needed to do was catch one.

15. *night*

The classroom was dark as night. At the front, next to a movie screen, their instructor talked from a podium. An old owl, blown down from a pine, he wore gold rimmed spectacles on the tip of his beak. They glinted in the projector light. Sometimes the owl would raise a wing to point at the next slide. Angels circling a holy woman. Florence, Venice, Rome. Gypsum was going to lectures, taking notes, writing essays, thinking, thinking, thinking.

16. *comedy*

By the end of the quarter, Maria and Gypsum had chairs in the back of the classroom. He liked laughing with her. She lived in the room across from Moose and they walked to class together. Something one of them whispered in the lecture started them laughing. Gypsum couldn't stop, he was crying from whatever that joke was. "Is there a problem?" the owl interrupted. "Yes, there is…" Gypsum wanted to say. It was so rare that you could laugh at something they were taught, a joke could set you off like a bomb. "Comedy!" Gypsum would try to explain.

17. *the town*

When the tide went out, the town appeared. A path made of flat stones led to it. Not far, a few hundred yards away, but you were surrounded by the low-tide mud, sand, and weeds. You wouldn't want to fall off that slick path, or be caught when the water came rushing back in. The gondolas wired overhead were a safer way to travel, but Gypsum liked to be part of the sea. He reached for shells. Once he found an old penny that someone must have dropped from a boat. Soon, the flagstones became concrete again, Main Street, Molasses Records, the bank, the Shop 'N' Save, the Woolworths, the movie theater, his favorite bookstores, and the houses crowded around.

18. *bookstores*

There were two amazing bookstores in town, Gulf Stream and Old Books. Gulf had the cutting edge best of the underground. Books you've never heard of with punk rock lyrics and strange magazines. That was Sacco's favorite place, of course. But Gypsum loved Old Books. It was across from the movie theater, in a brick building. A simple wooden sign. You had to go up steep stairs that creaked. The crooked hallway at top leaned to the left and right. It looked like that scene in *Invasion of the Body Snatchers* when they hide in an office. Every footstep was another creaking board. A painted flowery wavy sign above the door said Old Books. A big room filled with hundreds of books. A cardigan cat at the counter, a poster of the Marx Brothers on the wall. Another room led Gypsum to Steinbeck, Salinger, Walker Percy, Brautigan.

Old Books 7/27 19 64

M 136 Maine Street

No. Brunswick, Maine 04011

Reg. No. ______ Clerk ______	ACCOUNT FORWARDED		
1	Heller – Hasen	Hd v	3	00
2	Steinbach – Short			
3	Novel	Hd	2	50
4	Steinbeck – Grapes			
5	Wrath	Sat	2	75
6				
7			7	25
8				
9	Tax			37
10				
11			7	62
12				
13				
14				
15	48			

19. *wander*

Sometimes he let his mind wander during those lectures, or it's possible the pen he was using wasn't interested in taking notes anymore. It wanted to draw and write story ideas. This was just the sort of unpolished magic that Magic Island wanted him to hone into something of value.

20. *turning*

Winter was coming. Leaves were turning yellow and red. Gypsum had seen pictures of Magic Island covered in snow and you could feel it was coming. His grandmother met him in town where she was shopping, and he sat beside her in the station wagon on the way to dinner. Guernsey Road was posted at 45 mph, but she would drive as slow as 30 with cars stacking up behind. She didn't mind. Now she was cooking fish on the oil stove and Gypsum was in their cold bedroom, looking out the window. Pines and bramble. The hill dropped fast into the dark green water. He could see a blue heron wading slowly along the edge in the last pale bit of daylight.

Drawn in college notebook margin

21. *feeling*

What is that feeling? Knowing you're worth something nobody else can see. You can walk through walls of lecture halls, kick at leaves. No one hears when you make a song out of the cold temperature and play it like an orchestra on a floating cloud.

22. *snow*

The first snow arrived at night. They were walking back from the dining hall, heading back to Jekyll Hall. Snow had already started to quilt the paths. Big snowflakes fell in a hurry through the orange light of the lampposts. Windows in dorms were yellow and green. There were people shouting all around. Magic Island was going crazy. Pretty soon snowballs started to fly. It seemed inevitable as the Peloponnesian War. Gypsum, Louie, and Moose were caught in the middle. Three silhouettes leaned from a third-floor window, jumping around. It took Gypsum a few snowballs to get one through.

23. *thompson street*

Thompson Street branched off Main. Five minutes to find his grandmother's house. Brown shingles and butter colored trim. Her little blue car in the driveway. Her garden cut down for the cold. The screen door was elbowed with a spring that he would bend open to knock on the next door's window. He could see her in the kitchen. She would let him into a hug. He took his usual seat at the round table. She would put on hot water to make instant coffee from a jar. The newspaper was open on the table and she always had something to say.

24. *electric and moonlit*

In the winter, because of wind and ice, or whatever other bad weather was holding them back, the gondolas stopped working. Gypsum would take the ferryboat. It was a nice change. He liked to hold onto the rail, breathing in the ocean air, feeling the sting off the waves. He would look over the edge and stare at cold green water. He knew they were down there out of sight. Different schools of fish bunching together. He knew the feeling, he bounced between them. He was a minnow who went from this place to that. Just when friends thought they knew him and believed they could count on him to be around, he was gone. For Gypsum, it was all about imagination. Whoever sparked that, he wanted to be around. By being electric and moonlit he was able to experience being alive. Gypsum was becoming a writer, learning all the flavoring, the search for inspiration, loneliness and words looking for him, working their way into him, wanting to live on paper.

25. *confidence*

He had confidence there were books waiting for him to write. He already finished one novel and was working on a second. The rejection letters would come to his grandparents' house. His grandmother would call him, and he would go there to see what Doubleday or Random House had to say. It was okay if they didn't want him. He would tell himself, that's part of being a writer, getting through these rough times before you make it.

26. *match*

Gypsum made a name for himself on the first floor of Jekyll Hall. He decorated the door with collage, drawings and stories and a weekly horoscope. He painted a mural on the wall in watercolors. And so it happened that Frisco up on the fifth floor heard of him. Gypsum found a friend who made movies, also liked the music of Sir Victor Uwaifo, and had humor to match. After all, for his photo in the new student guide, Frisco stared into the camera with a rat on his shoulder.

```
YOUR FORTUNE:

    A MAN BEARING SIX OYSTERS WILL OFFER YOU HIS SERVICE...
```

27. *adaptation*

A better narrator would have included more Frisco in this book. A better narrator might have made him the star instead of Gypsum Tweed. The two of them certainly had their share of escapades worthy of a bestseller book with a much-anticipated movie adaptation in the works. Bowing to that editorial pressure, this stubborn narrator promises to include more.

28. *broken*

The four years packed together like a snowball. He didn't know it at the time, but every day was melting a little more in his hand. Or maybe he did know, maybe he felt it all along, maybe that's why he was the way he was. Seemingly he knew he was making memories, but how could he realize they would be seen by us? In his second year, Gypsum had a roommate who wanted to be a dentist. All he ever did was study, sitting in his neat, narrow room surrounded by a tidy stack of books, with the desk lamp on. Magic Island was just a waiting room, playing the dreariest music, while he sat and turned pages underlined with a yellow pen. The tantalizing future where he would have his name on a door in a Midwest business park was still years ahead.

29. *records*

Frisco's roommate had a record collection of marching bands. They would drive Frisco crazy. The microphone was set up at the fifty-yard line and every time the brassy formation turned, the sound would fade like geese in a cold sky. Then all of a sudden, they would spin again toward the grandstand and the microphone would catch them full blast with the theme to *Rocky* or some familiar TV jingle. Meanwhile, Gypsum and Frisco went to the Goodwill in town to hunt for records. They became familiar with the albums and singles that never made it past the past. It's a story old as Eskimos returning to their ice-covered rooms with a paper bag full of fresh ghosts for the jukebox.

30. *adventure*

Andrei Tarkovsky visited Magic Island. He arrived in a stamped pine box. Frisco invited him and the old master actually arrived—all the way from Russia! Frisco painted a banner that stretched across the wall in the dining hall. They couldn't believe it was happening. That night Tarkovsky filled the movie screen in the Museum of Art. It was magic how Frisco managed that feat, he got things like that done. He always had an adventure up his sleeve. Like the time they wheeled a VW engine into the Colds Tower elevator, up to Frisco's room to work on. Or the time they went to the fourth floor of the Science Building and climbed a ladder into the attic. He showed them the roofbeams by flashlight. Messages were written up there, some as old as time, and they reached and added their own.

31. *competition*

Every winter a clam chowder competition was held at Guernsey or Thompson Street. Gypsum's grandparents would each have a pot warming on the stove. His grandfather never failed to mention his rival's potatoes. He would hold up a spoon and say, "How on earth did you cut these potatoes so perfectly? They're all the same size..." He was convinced she was using some sort of witchcraft, or she was buying them cubed from the Shop N' Save frozen aisle. Gypsum didn't mind. He sat at a table with two bowls and enjoyed dinner and a show.

32. *okay*

There was a poolroom in the Union. Gypsum liked to go there with his friends and pretend to be some Mississippi shark. When he played badly it was only a ruse. "I meant to do that." Once he left to go make a call. His favorite phonebooth was down the hall in the shadow of the stairs, standing there like Humphrey Bogart. It was made of 1940s oak and had a door like a treehouse. Gypsum called home and asked about his dog and caught up on the news. Everything was okay. When he hung up, a fountain of quarters spilled from the coin return. He had to cup his hands underneath then use his coat to catch them all. Suddenly he was rich. Rich enough to treat his friends in the poolroom to whatever they wanted from the vending machine.

33. *attraction*

Marjorie lived on the third floor. She was crying and carrying on. He sat with her and listened to The English Beat. It was a dramatic time for her, she had just broken up with her boyfriend. Gypsum had seen the guy. He couldn't understand the attraction. He couldn't understand how she could shipwreck over some dumbbell like that. The call of being blue was too much. With so many sad songs she could play on the record player and fall into like a never-ending well.

34. *halls and shadows*

Gypsum watched *The Cabinet of Doctor Caligari* fifty-two times. That might be a school record. When he was writing an essay on German Expressionism, he knew every frame of that movie. He followed those bent painted halls and shadows as if it was his very own dream. Bergman, Herzog, Wenders, Fellini, those dreams in the film library were as welcome to him as the songs in Gibson Hall. That's where he would check out headphones and *Music of the Rain Forest Pygmies*. Closing his eyes, he was no longer in the library. The wooden chair and table and record player carried him floating, deeper into the jungle.

35. *blurred*

The girl with one eye caught his attention. Gypsum worked up the nerve to ask her out. She was quiet and nervous as a deer and wore long black dresses and he would do anything to see her smile. They walked to Morningstar Cinema, not far from the gondolas. The streets of town were still piled with snow. The sidewalk had a crisp layer of ice. He made a joke about a dogsled taxi to take them home. She said something almost silently. It was a cold walk to see a movie about a boy who could fly. The trees blurred underneath him. He winged her back to her room and blurred from her the same way.

36. *discontent*

I've noticed a lot of discontent among the memory machine workers. One of them stopped me at the water cooler and explained that she wasn't the only one dismayed with Gypsum Tweed. I understand. I keep reminding the staff—there's nothing else we can do but observe and record impartially. Let's face it, if things didn't happen the way they did, this book wouldn't even exist. None of them would have this job. This narrator would be doing something different too. I might be selling balloons in the park. I might not exist at all.

37. *mistakes*

I won't admit it to the staff, but it's true, it isn't easy for this narrator to go back in time like this. Watching these memories is more than a crystal ball can bear, it actually takes a toll. This was an age when Gypsum Tweed thought he knew what it was all about. Didn't everyone at Magic Island? He was learning that he was learning, and making mistakes was part of that. There are times when this narrator wants to yell at Gypsum like the Ghost of Christmas Yet to Come, but that's no use, I can't reach him, nobody's there. Even if we could contact him, figure out a way to warn him, perhaps in a dream, what would be the point? Everybody knows the rule in time-travel: changing one little thing affects the entire future. There is no way to intrude. Besides, the job of Jiminy Cricket is already taken.

38. *view of the trees*

Often as he could, Gypsum would visit his grandparents.
Once he brought along his art history book and gave them a
lecture on Mondrian. He sounded like an owl. He also brought
the books he was reading in the William Faulkner class. Later
on, his grandfather would be lying down in that cold room
with the view of the trees and the dark sky. The green bedside
lamp is on. He's reading *The Sound and the Fury*.

fun
fun

39. *celebrity*

For a little while, maybe a week, Gypsum Tweed wore sunglasses. They weren't the sort you would expect to see on a celebrity in *The World Weekly News*. He bought them downstairs at Woolworths. Or maybe they were from Mammoth Mart. They were cheap toy sunglasses meant for a kid, white plastic, with bright stickers around the lenses that spelled out FUN FUN. Somehow they attracted the attention of a girl who sat with him in the dining hall. He felt like a different person. She was a Bio-Chemistry major and tired from studying all the time. She needed all the fun she could find. Did she really think those words were genuine? Could he live up to them, be fun, fun all the time? The pressure of deep water was too much for his submarine.

40. *reason*

Nighttime and he is on a porch at Omega Psi. Not that he
wanted to join. Gypsum Tweed avoided official groups and
recognitions, everything he did was below the radar and always
would be. This book is the bones of an unknown archaeopteryx.
Music is coming from inside a dark room with dancing and red
lights. Jonathan Richman. What would college be without this
scene, after all it was in every movie. He couldn't escape. The
smoke and fumes were after him, they would follow him, catch
him and carry him. He followed a path back to shore, he felt
like lying down in the slick weeds and being carried out by the
tide. He didn't know why he kept going on. There must have
been a reason.

41. *sound effects*

Gypsum had a radio show on Sunday afternoon. That put him on right after the hockey game. And he had a plan. He had a couple sound effect records from the music library. Two tracks were all he needed. As Gypsum dialed back the thrilling conclusion of Rick Tombs' sports program, he became Orson Welles. The record on turntable 1 started. He allowed the roar of a crowd to return. That sound effect was only a minute long, he would have to be quick. "Yes, radio listeners," he mimicked Rick's delivery, "That was quite a game, wasn't it? Nearly won this time." The cheering had thirty seconds to go. "Hey! Look who's walking onto the ice! It's the college president. He's waving to the crowd. Hello, Elroy!" Next, Gypsum started the second record. There was only one sound. A gunshot. "Oh no!" Gypsum cried. He conjured up the Hindenburg, "Oh the humanity!" Then seamlessly, he let the crowd noise fade into a Miles Davis song.

42. *haunted*

Michelle told him she lived in a haunted house. Gypsum knew the place, he had been past it many times, an old white painted farmhouse. It looked like a painting by Winslow Homer. The fields rolled around her in waves. She said she would wake up at night sometimes and see a woman standing by the dresser. Michelle and Gypsum might have had a class together, that detail is unclear, but however it happened, they liked to see each other. And *Oh!* how he wanted to spend the night with her in that room.

43. *the otherworld*

What happened to the other people he knew for a little while? We don't even have all their names. We know they were there. It would take a master hypnotist to see into the otherworld and find them. For instance, Gypsum was in the inner circle of a pop band. He was often at their apartment and he went to their shows. The kind of shows played in cellars and city bars. Cover songs by Squeeze, The Cure, Violent Femmes. Where do you hear that music now? Supermarkets, department stores, on TV movies. He wanted to be with a girl like Cyndi Lauper. We've seen the evidence, we heard him sing her songs on the radio.

44. *rumor*

Professor Elliot had a piano idea. A Steinway was rolled from Gibson to Colds Tower. He walked behind it like a pharaoh, offering helpful suggestions as it was heaved towards the elevator. He entered first and it took three students to wedge the piano in around him. His TA pressed RECORD and the tape-deck began to turn. The piano keys rang, the doors shut, the chains heaved all that weight up and down in the shaft for half an hour. It's not known if *Music for Elevators* really happened, but that was the rumor.

So instead of a definite vote of those in favour of
~~Liberal~~ Labour + those for **C**onservative, the 'same'
column, which a large percentage of people use,
has altered the totals. Therefore I've decided
to add the 'same' column percentage to the
party being dealt with.) Because of the ~~Some of the same column~~ phrasing of the question',
a misrepresentation is inevitable.) Unemployment
is closely related to strikes, so a similarity
in   voter response is not unexpected.

It would be best to assume that the voting
on unemployment remained much the same in
both voting elections. For example ~~the~~ the total
vote that Conservatives would better control unemployment)
in 1974 was 22.4% (~~and~~ or 56.9% with the 'same' vote) and
while in 1979, this vote was 50.5% feeling
of Conservative adequacy for the job. ~~Some of the~~
~~same vote would go to~~ The percentages, with the
same vote added are much the same. If anything, one would expect

Allen Frost
English 230
3/16/88

MOTORCYCLE QUARTET

Jonson and Easy Rider

ALLEN FROST
HISTORY 1

WHEN YOU'RE OSTRACIZED, WHO
FORWARDS YOUR LUGGAGE ??

nice
title,
I lika it

Allen Frost
Art History 252
November 30, 1986

THERE WAS A CROOKED MAN
A Study of The Cabinet of Doctor Caligari as
Expressionist Art

45. *the collected essays*

The Collected Essays of Gypsum Tweed will not be required reading at Harvard. It's only by some miracle that they still exist. There must have been a preserving spell involved. Looking through them, our team of researchers (this narrator included) are constantly surprised. Gypsum was daring wild things with essays. At that time, Magic Island didn't have creative writing classes, so Gypsum forged strange essay/story hybrids that lurched and snapped, like the creatures made by Doctor Moreau.

Summer had nearly ended, with school beginning once again.
Trees still held tight to their green leaves though cold breezes
would blow them at night. It was one of those nights then...
    "It was the book that caused me to fall asleep so quickly.
Nearly 11:00 was when <u>The Romance of the Rose</u> cast its comatic
spell on me and collapsed me into stupor. A noise shook me from
my sleep, as if the Rockettes were high-kicking their way down
the hall and offstage into the night. Anyway, that stampede
woke me up and I looked out my window and saw in the distance,
a building lit like it was full daylight.

Above, parody of Jonathan Swift

Below, Willie Mays destroys an essay

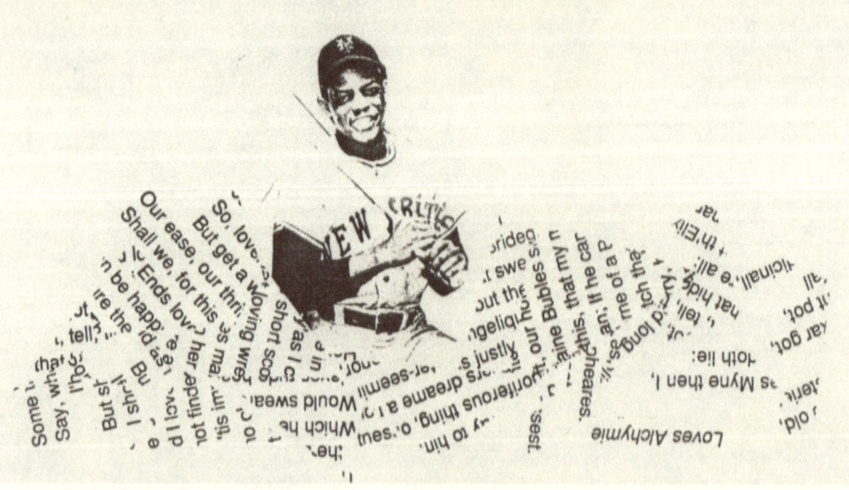

66

7. A Mad Tea-Party

Andrew Marvell sitting there dreaming of "The Garden," his Wonderland Eden, while Alice falls into hers. Marvell has his ideas of nature (sanctified, pure, ideal) and with Edenic visions would walk through that green. But if he were to stumble into (to see with Alice's eyes) Carroll's Wonderland, he would be confronted with a very different nature.

Marvell finds society attempting to approximate a resemblance of nature, setting as its highest honors those things found in the garden.

> She had not gone much farther before she came in sight of the house of the March Hare: she thought it must be the right house, because the chimneys were shaped like ears and the roof was thatched with fur.

His poem reasons that the features of nature are something to be imitated, yet the strivings of man to hope to gain something of nature's glory (as symbolized by laurels) are impossible. The garden (Eden) has rejected humankind and their mourning of that perfection gone is this poem's concern--a sense of longing the lost.

> The March Hare took the watch and looked at it gloomily: then he dipped it into his cup of tea, and looked at it again: but he could think of nothing better to say than his first remark, 'It was the best butter, you know.'

46. *not a word*

And let's not forget "Essay is a Saddlesore," narrated by a college student attempting to write about the 17th century. The endeavor crashes to a halt as the dorm room is invaded by country musicians (Patsy Cline, Hank Williams, Johnny Cash, etc.) and the poor student struggles to continue for the next ten pages with them interrupting his scholarly composition. He explains, "Part of being an English major is the total devaluing of the beauty and excitement of language—that's why we write essays!" He swears and begs them to leave, "I'm gonna get a Pass grade again! Everything was going so well before you showed up! I had my outline all ready...I'm to page 5 and I haven't said a thing since page 1!" The essay is peppered with comments from the teacher like "not a word," "unidiomatic," "unintelligible."

ESSAY IS A SADDLESORE

"Okay, great here we go--an essay on the perpetuation of sexual frustration from the Restoration era literature to today." He rubs his hands, blows some air between his thumbs, hot friction palms together, wildly excited with the prospects of his essay as only an English major can be. "First an outline, then I'll start writing...it's always good to have an outline to write from. Get my thoughts down on paper. All right.":

Intro.: The perception of women as seen in Restoration Literature
as a negative image.

    A. The poetry of Swift exemplifying a prominent writing man's
view of women. His perception of women as seen in his poem,
'The Progress of Beauty.' Male opinions of Female.

    B. The feminist writings of Mary Montagu, a contemporary of Swift but a
contrasting positive view of women. Female opinions of Male.

    C. Views of woman in popular American culture today. Still no understanding between
the sexes. Misunderstanding between Female and Male, pitting themselves
against each other for no reason other than inbred societal misconceptions.

Conclusion: It is scary how little has changed with the hundreds of years of Western society in
the views of women despite the feminist calling for a more equal society. Things
cannot get better until the sexes realize how much they share in common.

"Excellent, we're all set to go." Pen in hand, he began to write:

One notes certain cultural values pertaining to and reflecting societal views in the writings of the authors of the Restoration era. Indeed, the most prominent of these views is the equating of women with baser qualities than men.

Swift represents an extreme reaction to the societal view of women. Societal values viewed women in an unrealistic way, treating them as inferior mentally to men, but also as beings who were somehow unworldly creatures and delicate, purely beautiful things. Swift sees through this untruth, but takes an extremist view in his representation of women. In his poem, 'The Progress of Beauty,' Swift reveals this opinion:

> *To see her from her pillow rise,*
>
> *All reeking in a cloudy steam,*
>
> *Crack'd lips, foul teeth, and gummy eyes,*
>
> *Poor Strephon, how would he blaspheme! (Lines 13-16).*

Swift's view of women is antithetical to society's praise of women as beautiful objects, but he agrees with a vehemence in regards to women's inferiority to men.

There was a crash on the door behind him, and instinctively he dove under his desk, woodchips showering, flying from the shattered door hinge. He cowered there in the shadows, hugging his knees, closing tight his eyes. And the room suddenly smelled of leather and rawhide bootstraps and mud chaps and the stale smell of an August prairee wind. There was alcohol and cigarettes, chili breaths and chuckwagon dragged aromas and through the window, a high plains drifter moon and stars and he heard crickets although it was 23 degrees outside...He felt the presense of cowboys behind him...There was a stampede-holler yelp yodel as he turned terrified to look and see what had entered so intrudingly and uninvited. A herd of cowboys stood just inside the doorway to his room. The yodel came again, this time with an introduction, "It's Gene Autry! King of the Singing Cowboys!"

"What the hell is-!" the student started but stopped in shock as the cowboys parted into two even ranks and down the middle marched Gene Autry, resplendent matinee idol, wearing a red and black satin cowboy suit with stars and with a big ten gallon white hat to top it off. Coming from the six sting guitar he carried in his arms came a song, warbling off his lips came these words:

Oh, listen to that rhythm of the range,

47. *publication*

"Essay is a Saddlesore" was Gypsum's first publication, posted on the row of trees in front of Hawthorne Hall. What possessed him to do that? The production crew and I had to watch the memory machine a few times, especially the part when Gypsum Tweed tells the teacher where to find his essay. The nerve of that kid! And he couldn't believe it when people on the path stopped to read it. Suddenly his writing was famous! A senior dressed like Lou Reed told him it was great.

48. *filled with hours*

What was it like to fly in a jet airliner seven miles above Earth? It was a long time sitting. Reading. Thinking. Restless overhead speakers ping or crackle with announcements. Turbulence. Snacks. He remembered a time when smoking was allowed and the back of the plane was a cloud. Gypsum tore open the courtesy earphones bag. Plug the cord in the armrest like an astronaut and listen to Beethoven, or dial Mel Brooks on another channel. The window shows clouds. Everything is slow motion out there. A stewardess pushes a silver cart down the aisle. It doesn't smell like flowers. Gypsum gets hot tea. The sky is filled with hours. Finally, there are mountains below. Gypsum rubs his ears. The plane is slowly descending. Magic Island is far away in the other direction like an unseen kite at the end of a long string.

49. *cotton*

Across the water from the island, up the rocky shore, past all the stores and the park, at the end of Main Street, the abandoned mill was frozen. Well into spring, the ice clung to its waterwheel. The cotton hasn't spun for thirty years. Broken windows. Haunted smudges. Brick smokestacks. Vines are growing over. It won't even take a century to be a fairytale crumble. It's best not to go that far down the street, go no further than LaVerdiere's pharmacy, play it safe. Magic has limits out in the world. There are families in town who had children who worked in the mill and teenagers who went straight to the factory looms from school and they never got out til they were old, if they were lucky.

50. *the piano*

One day in the middle of winter, Gypsum found a piano. Why was there a piano cut off from the world, alone in the Union? It could have been the same piano Elliot played in the elevator. Now it looked like an old horse in a cold stable. There were no lights on, it was getting later in the afternoon, the window was gray and white. Who knows why he opened the sliding door and went in? The piano was holding its breath, waiting for someone like him to come along.

51. *celestial*

The wooden telephone booth was an antique old as Rome. Gypsum felt like he was in a bus station in 1949 Kansas. He would line the quarters on the bench seat and pick up that heavy black receiver, hear the buzz of an electric beehive, and dial three thousand miles away. Being in this little wooden church was comforting. Even when he heard the news that his dog had died. He sat in that celestial booth and cried. The thought appeared that he would never see her again, not in this world.

52. *hypnosis*

A rainy dark evening with nothing to do, a hypnotist came to school. He reeled them in. The gym bleachers were full of students. He strutted back and forth across the polished floor with a microphone in hand, bad jokes and bravado, the opposite of the instructors, this guy had been on *The Tonight Show* and casino stages. Then he called for volunteers and sat them behind him in folding chairs. He warned his audience that it was just possible that, "others of you, suggestable to hypnosis, may go under too." Gypsum fought the temptation and watched as the subjects became chickens. The hypnotist gathered eggs from them, holding each one up for the audience to see. That would have been okay, until he dropped one of the eggs and gagged at the rotten smell. He choked on every horrible word he could think of to describe the odor and suddenly a chicken leaped off its chair and bolted. As the hypnotist commanded someone to catch it, the chicken crashed through the exit and ran into the winter night. It's possible they're still out there, running.

53. *magic*

In his Junior year, Gypsum met Jed. Frisco sent a letter from Thailand and said they should meet. And he was right, the two of them became thick as thieves. It's funny how that happens. Jed had a hydroplane. They could explore up and down the coast. They ran an hour away to Waterville to see *Sid and Nancy*. They would skid out into the blacktop night beyond the harbor, roaring to Portland and further destinations too. Magic Island was losing its hold. They listened to Joy Division and Justin Hinds. They could talk all day and night and laugh to beat the band. Wasn't finding a friend all about unseen magnetic levels, finding worlds you never knew, and if that wasn't magic what was? Despite all the essays and tests and droll in the classroom atmosphere, maybe the school was teaching magic after all.

54. *music*

Soon after that, Romulus moved into the apartment. Now it was Gypsum, Jed, Sacco, and Romulus. Romulus was returning from Nepal. He wore a long green quilted coat that he bought in Kathmandu. "The door swung open and a fig newton entered." The Beatles, The Feelies, John Cage with a ladle of Captain Spaulding. Romulus was a guitar player. It was funny how music was so much in their air—they could sit in a room and listen for hours. You could find lyrics in a song that meant more than Plato. Gypsum was thrown for another loop. Can you believe amazing people are all around you?

55. *other radios*

Their radio show was a collage of sounds, skipping records, and spontaneous comedy scenarios. It was a miracle Romulus and Gypsum could send those signals far across the pines and water into town, as far as they would reach and vanish. Walking home at night, they liked to point at the stars and be glad their program was on its way. Passing satellites and planets and moons. Somewhere out there were other radios, other beings listening in wonder and delight as Kenny Rogers stuttered the same word over and over again, needle stuck in a vinyl groove, awash in a background of sound.

56. *unexpected*

Another one of the priceless treasures excavated for this book is a contraption you don't see much anymore. Few people at the radio station were aware that it was Gypsum Tweed's handiwork. *Fleas Please* was handwritten on an 8-track tape cartridge shelved next to the turntables with the other carts, advertisements, sponsors, and community alerts. But something unexpected happened if an unknowing DJ grabbed Fleas Please and plugged it in. "We'll be right back after this message," would be followed by an eerie twenty seconds of wolves howling in reverb.

57. *the back row*

"Welcome to *Jazz Talk* and our first listener. Hello, you're on the air."

"Yes, I have a question. What was Benny Goodman's favorite breakfast cereal?"

Then, just like that, *Jazz Talk* was banned. The teacher stopped lecturing and glared up the elevating seats, to the back row where Gypsum and Romulus were live at the microphone. They were still laughing. He asked them, "Could you two please keep it down?" No, they couldn't. Sorry. There was no way. They were the next Bob & Ray.

58. *greetings*

The resident advisor of the Mayflower Apartments had the key to a locked supply closet. And she had the difficult job of being their audience. A few times a month they knocked on her door to get more tissues or garbage bags and they made a one-act play out of the event. Each time, they took turns introducing Romulus as if he was newly arrived. There was always something mildly disturbing about him. His head was bandaged, or he was holding a fork and poking at the air. Once he was cradling a bowling ball adorned with a wig. Their greetings were sincere, the routine never changed, and she would only stare and say, "Yes, I've met him before."

59. *legacy*

Rib Eye Special was a short-lived, loud-head band Romulus, Sacco and Gypsum formed. The berserk songs were stuffed with straw, soaked in barnyard squeal. Gypsum played a thumping washtub bass and they howled idiot lyrics, Sacco sermons, punctuated with a shrill harmonica solo by Romulus. They were on the radio once. They performed live in the Union one eventful time. And that was legacy enough, wouldn't you think?

However, there was more. Not far from the shore where the gondolas touched down, along busy Bathtub Road, they were honored by the Chuck Wagon restaurant. The menu featured charcoal broiled sandwiches like The Saddletramp, The Cattle Drive, The Cowpoke's Delight, and of course their infamous Strawberry Short Cake. Then there was The Rib Eye Special: "¼ pound western steer served with golden lariats, hot buttermilk biscuits, tub butter, toss salad, cold water, and a dill pickle fresh from the barrel." It was like hearing the roar of the crowd, having a big-time sponsor, given keys to drive a high-powered racecar doomed to burn and blow up in the final heat.

Rockland, Livermore Falls, Lewiston and Brunswick.

60. *zen*

For a while Gypsum was a campus daredevil. Below the ground, on the ground, in the air. It was Frisco's idea to climb the Chapel tower. While a musical lecture on Zen proceeded calmly in the church nave, Frisco opened a thin door hidden behind a curtain and led the way. A hundred ten feet of wooden ladder crept straight up into the black. The narrow stone shaft echoed with the spidery sound of a koto. The ladder creaked. Halfway to the top, a dim glow flowed. Gypsum could see the audience far below, through a grating. Light and shadow fell over him in stripes like one of those film noir detectives. The ladder chirped as Frisco continued ascending. Gypsum saw a girl turn around and stare. He froze, clawed tight to the pine rung, willing himself to be unseeable as Zen.

61. *rabbits*

The first time they met Hater, they were in the steam tunnels under campus. His flashlight shined down into the manhole and they could hear him order the other security guard to follow them. She told him not a chance and they laughed and scurried on like rabbits. They found a tunnel that came out in a classroom. Fit snug in the wall like a door in The Hardy Boys. Another night, Jed and Gypsum were comically caught sneaking into the swimming pool, and twenty minutes later Hater found them again, on the roof of the library. Was it a rebellious streak, or was Gypsum just being a fool? He was keeping his guardian angel busy. Anyway, these were the sorts of crazed adventures that would be left behind—it was safer for a writer to imagine things like this on paper.

62. *philosophy*

Gypsum's grades took a turn for the worse when he took "Introduction to Philosophy." The instructor was a wizard with a long white beard who wore a baggy robe, sneakers, and black rimmed glasses with thick lenses that magnified his rheumy eyes. Gypsum had to visit his office. One big sneeze in there would've made a paper tornado. The teacher held Gypsum's essay then dropped it between them on the desk. He told Gypsum, "You have trouble writing, don't you?" The painting could have fallen off the wall. Gypsum was speechless. It took him a moment. It reminded Gypsum of the rejection letters he got. He knew he needed to be stronger when that happened. It was only someone else's judgement. There was nothing clairvoyant about that teacher's question, no amount of philosophy had made the old man any wiser.

63. *real life*

He read in one of Sacco's underground guidebooks that a writer needed the harsh participation in the world. That was something Gypsum thought about. Magic Island was a safe little bubble, a dream, but no special protected world exists for writers. The so-called real world would come sweeping in like the tide. They must be released into it like salmon. Gypsum Tweed was convinced suffering made an artist. Get used to washing dishes, factory assembly lines and timeclock jobs. Then everything that happened would be material for books and stories. Real life would deliver the experiences for imagination. Being a writer was like being the man shot out of a circus cannon—you were only made aware by the dangers and transitory spectacle of life. Ridiculous!

64. *joy and adventure*

It's easy for us to see where he was going wrong. Here in this unseen future, separated from Gypsum Tweed by another dimension, we wish we could step in. But he was intent on going his own way, guided by some other narrator and crew who would have a lot more to do than us.

After years of being in the business, it's been this narrator's experience that art is magic, it comes from beyond. It doesn't matter where you are or what you're doing—if it's meant to find you, it will. And you know what? Truthfully, being a writer isn't even a job anymore, an author who makes a living from books is as rare as some tropical bird on ice-skates. My advice to Gypsum would be find a job like mine that pays the bills, that isn't entirely unpleasant to work at, while all the while you write when you get the chance. Don't worry about publishers and rejections. Be your own publisher! The future will find you. We did!

Oh, and one more thing—inspiration doesn't need pain. Sure, there are famous exceptions, Poe and Baudelaire, but Gypsum Tweed wasn't made for that. Gypsum Tweed had no lack of inspiration, he had people around him who brought him joy and adventure and stories that rolled in the air. He didn't have to make life hard for himself.

65. *successful*

A posting on the job board directed Gypsum to the dining hall. He and Sacco had seen the lanky guy with the ponytail before, standing on the loading dock in back, smoking a cigarette. Sacco had already named him Metallica. Now it was up to Metallica whether to hire Gypsum for the kitchen crew. Metallica didn't seem to care one way or the other. But with that decision, Gypsum felt the first successful step towards his goal. He felt stories growing all around him. The walk across campus, the loading dock where Metallica left a coffee tin of crushed cigarettes, the employee's entrance, through the dented door, getting his card for the timeclock. Into the steam of where he worked. A silver track of conveyor rollers brought dishes to the kitchen. Gypsum imagined this as a science fiction. Stories were piling up like plates and coffee cups.

66. *ideas*

Where do your ideas come from? There's a question Gypsum would have heard a lot as an author. I can tell you the answer. Memories, Dreams, Inspirations are located here. We send them through the air.

We exist in another world. Our office is a small house between Dreams and Memories. The third department, Inspirations, is a castle on the other side of the lake. They have direct contact with their subject, they send them ideas that turn into something marvelous. Ideas are important, they keep humanity evolving. Some ideas will change the world. Someone like Einstein or the Buddha had entire floors at Inspirations working overtime.

Whoever was assigned to Gypsum Tweed had a quiet wooden desk by a window. Whoever was sitting there only had to find Gypsum Tweed and tune in. But allow me to mention, whoever was broadcasting to Gypsum Tweed was no big-top promoter. I would say the radio dial was tuned to the same sort of narrator who spoke to Emily Dickinson. Gypsum Tweed strayed from the limelight. We're only beginning to discover him all these years later.

67. *inspiration*

The memory machine is housed in a simple little building at the end of a gravel drive.

I was asked to do a book on Gypsum Tweed—it was more of a dare really—to recreate what could be recovered from the past. At first, I didn't think it could be done. But we have a good crew. I'm the first one here in the morning. I unlock the door, I make coffee, I turn on the machine. I say hello to the volunteers as they come in and then I just stay out of their way until the end of the day. When everyone is gone, I hold the pages and go outside onto the doorstep overlooking the water. On either side of me there are houses and trees, the windmills, the aqueduct, and the radio towers broadcasting inspiration.

68. *melting*

Gypsum preferred the smaller cafeteria in the Union. It was more comfortable than the airport atmosphere in the big dining hall near Colds Tower. He liked to get a cup of tea and read *On the Road*. Time passed. Magic Island was melting. Winter was fading. Ponds were starting to form across the walkways and if you weren't careful crossing Main Street, you could step into a deep stream. There were birds in those tall stark trees, singing them into spring leaves.

69. *style*

She walked across campus in pajamas, boots, and a sheepskin coat. Gypsum admired her style. That was quite a statement, but if there was anything he wanted to tell her, he could only yell. Jed claimed her father was an actor in the sci-fi movie, *Lazarus Pun*. Her father's job in the 22nd century was hunting society's fugitives known as Punners, shouting at them from the floating walkways and the chase was on. Gypsum found inspiration in that future world. He and Jed hid themselves behind a holly and Gypsum yelled, "Punner!" He couldn't see her through the sharp leaves. He asked Jed, "Did she look?"

70. *girls*

Let's face it, there wasn't a lot Gypsum Tweed knew about girls. He liked being around them, he liked to see them laugh, hear them talk, and he liked the way everything changed when you liked one. They seemed a lot more magical than most of his studies. He registered for "Romantic Poetry of the 19th Century." He tried to register for "Love Potions," but it was full. He had to take "Talking to Ghosts" instead. Things would have been different if he got in the love potions class, he was sure of that.

71. *together*

How did he meet Agatha Mersey? They were close all this time, orbiting, just missing one another. Magic Island was only so big, and he was bound to run into her. Both worked for dining services, but she worked in the Union. How many times around campus did he pass her by? He asked her, "How did I never see you?" She said, "I don't know, you were always looking somewhere else." If this was a movie, you would see them together, walking between buildings, meeting in the library, sitting in a booth at the Union. That's where she said, "I can ask my supervisor to transfer you to this cafeteria, if you want." That would be great! He could work back in the kitchen, but he could see her whenever he got the chance. She stood at the register and waved at him.

72. *happy*

They liked to have tea in the Union. He would carry their cups together on a tray. The cashier waved them through. The old wooden dining hall felt like they were in Europe, or in one of those 1930s New York hotels. Fred Astaire and Ginger Rogers danced around them. Who knows what they were talking about? They were happy. When they left, they would stop to check the mail. He loved that Automat wall of glass and gold metal. Maybe there's a ghost of him around those mailboxes. It's possible Magic Island will honor old 311, have a miniature sign attached to it, commemorating the days it belonged to Gypsum Tweed. He loved to go there with Agatha. He liked to see her become a safecracker, opening the little door to find a letter. Sometimes they sent each other letters. What a thrill to find one. Everyone was hoping for the same thing, what those two had.

73. *so long*

He felt like he was catching up with her on all the years he didn't know her. They talked about books, *Harriet the Spy, From the Mixed-Up Files of Mrs. Basil E. Frankweiler, June 30th, June 30th.* She laughed when he sang from her copy of *The Hobbit.* They remembered their favorite scenes in *The Pink Panther Strikes Again.* He didn't know why it took so long to find her.

Remember, I was the one who recommended
a Confederacy of Dunces + that was great.

74. *2:22*

Somehow, he ended up in her room a lot. They would talk and laugh and play records and read from her books. Edward Gorey and Pete Seeger and Flannery O'Connor. She liked to stay up late, that's how he found out about the clock. She explained that anytime you notice the time is 2:22, you have to say "Ooooh!" She hooted like an owl, and it was so funny he got the digital clock and reset the red numbers back a minute to hear her again. Maybe it was just being up that late that made the air rarified. He was probably in love with her and didn't even know it. The next time he was at Goodwill, he bought her a broken clock and glued the hands at 2:22 so it would stay that magic time forever.

75. *the moonflowers*

He noticed right away how much he liked sharing with
her what used to be the ordinary sights around Magic Island
and town. Nothing was the same anymore. Parked behind her
house, by the moonflowers and daylilies, she had a little car.
They would go to the bank together, and Shop N' Save, the
Post Office, Woolworths, and he would take her clomping up
those wooden stairs to Old Books. They drove half an hour to
Poplar Beach and landed on the sand. It was like the desert in
The Little Prince. They sat on a blanket in the dunes. She showed
him how to arrange the sand dollars, so they sing on the sand.
She started, "The time has come, the walrus said, to talk of
many things." He answered her, "Of shoes—and ships—
and sealing wax—of cabbages—and kings." And together
they sang it like a song, "And why the sea is boiling hot—and
whether pigs have wings!"

Allen—

Where are you?

I went to Smith Aud.

Find me there. ~~Here is~~
your ticket is w/ me or

76. *job posting*

At this point we lost another temp worker. She said she could see the writing on the wall. I have to agree with her, this project is temperamental at best. As I've explained, it affects me too. At this rate, I may have to post a job opening for a new narrator:

Title: Narrator

Category: Fiction

Description: Working closely with memories to edit and create an historical account. Working independently and in supervisory role, advising and instructing crew of researchers in equipment operation and application. Assist in building, constructing, forming and creating a work of art. Assist with care and maintenance of equipment and materials, according to safety regulations. Must be dependable and willing to work evenings and weekends.

This position requires:
- The ability to lift 50 lb. boxes of material
- Regular handling of archival materials some of which present a respiratory hazard
- The ability to work while experiencing emotional apprehension and misgivings
- The ability to operate some heavy machinery
- Manual dexterity with small hand tools
- Close attention to detail

Hours/Week: Full time

Pay Rate: Unpaid

Posted/Closed: Open until filled

77. *submissions*

Fur Stew magazine started in the library photocopier. Gypsum and his friends collaborated on stories and art. They ran fifty copies or so and left them in odd places. It was all anonymous, mysterious. On the back page were directions on where to leave submissions. "In Cupboard Hall on the 2nd floor you will find two portraits on the wall of our illustrious presidents Souls and Colds. Between them is a large throne. Open the door at the bottom of the chair and leave your creation under the mat." Imagine that—secret artists sneaking across campus! Cupboard Hall was built like a Gothic owl. Through the heavy castle door, up the white marble stairs, go like detectives carrying something wondrous.

78. *the printshop*

Miraculously, the school gave them a grant to publish more magazines. They were established! Now they could bring the page proofs to the campus printshop, where every issue was confronted with the problem of Hairbear and Deafy. (Credit is due to Sacco for those names). Hairbear darted in the back of the room where the smell of toner and ink was thickest. A prominent styled hairspray mane, gold-rimmed glasses, an impressive collection of disco shirts, you may have seen him in *Saturday Night Fever.* Gypsum and Sacco never spoke with him, their contact lurked at the counter. It never failed, every time they brought the next issue, the old man would wrinkle his face, hold a hand cupped to his ear and say, "Say again?"

79. *the stars*

Sacco was good at handing out names. Another new face at the Union was Carpetbagger. Gypsum laughed, but it was true. The new arrival really did have a carpetbag, sitting on the bench beside him. And he was always writing in a notebook, or drawing, or reading, everything that made him interesting to Sacco and Gypsum. They were both cagey though. It took Gypsum a week or so. Their first conversation was about black and white movies and Edgar Allan Poe. Carpetbagger wasn't a student—he was sent from the outside world. He would inspire them to be creative every day, as if their lives depended on it, as if they were the stars of a Super-8 movie that went on long past Magic Island.

80. *momentum*

Gypsum Tweed had a unique way of dismounting a bicycle. Here he was in action: riding straight at the Pickford Theater. He aimed for the bike rack then he just stepped backwards, off the pedals, and let the bike rattle forward by its own momentum until it clanged into the stand, caught between the rungs. Oblivious of the people watching him, he strolled to the door. He probably imagined himself an old cartoon cowboy with a metal horse that was done running across deserted plains and would wait for him outside the saloon.

81. *another wall*

These were the days of movie projectors when you would sit dark as underwater, below a light river, and watch W.C. Fields try to sleep on a balcony that filled the theater wall. He existed in a black and white dream. A broken beam, a falling bed, a clattering milkman, a coconut, LeFong, velocipede. Another time there was another wall, where nothing happened. The wall was the star of a notorious experimental film, a test of endurance that dared you to call it art. For half an hour, Gypsum stared at the blue wallpaper in a New York City apartment room. Thirty minutes where time stood still. W.C. Fields would have loved it.

82. *reading*

Senior year, on the second floor of the library, Gypsum Tweed had his own assigned desk. It was piled with books. He spent hours getting lost in those pages. There were cities and forests and rivers and deserts that reached into the distance. He had to write what he saw, what he thought about. And every once in a while, he had to come back. Then he stood up and walked along the carpet with the shelves rowing along beside him until he turned the corner and got to where Romulus was working. Once he caught sight of Gypsum, Romulus peered over his own sandbagged desk and pretended to be reading a book, upside-down.

MOOD METER '

FOR

THE LEE DUBOIS COURSE

IN

SELLING TECHNIQUES

BELONGS TO

Allen W. Frost, 26 Elm

FROM

AUTOCONDITIONING

The New Way to a Successful Life

by

HORNELL HART

Englewood Cliffs, N. J.

PRENTICE-HALL, INC.

83. *destined*

Gypsum Tweed was destined to be a writer, that had been the goal since third grade, he just didn't know how to make a living that way. It wasn't something they taught at Magic Island. To be fair, they tried. Sort of. They had a Job Fair day. Tables were set up in rows in the gym. Banners, balloons, brochures. The doorway was as close as Gypsum got to the corporate world. He just had the feeling he wasn't ready for that. He couldn't imagine being a salesman or working in an office. All that he learned had to be turned into a ten-hour day for Pine Oil or Penobscot Retail? What were these four years for? He turned around, went his own way. He had all this magic in him, he had to figure out on his own what to do with it.

84. *easy*

When Wordsworth and Coleridge were done for the day, the teacher returned Gypsum's essay and told him he should write for *The Tonight Show*. He tried to imagine that. Palm trees, sunshine, movie stars. Sleeping in a car in Burbank, showing up at the studio every day with a handful of jokes to pitch through the fence, waiting for his big break. The world wouldn't know what to do with him. His last day working in the kitchen at the Union, he told his boss goodbye and asked her for a job reference. She said, "You didn't spend your time here to be a dishwasher. You want to be an author, right?" Those words were so easy to say.

85. *experience*

Honestly, it's hard to know what was making him so blind. I guess it's like running around in circles with a flower no one can see. Did he want Instant Author? Available in powder form, only ten calories, served hot or cold, just add water. Did he think that potion existed? Why didn't he see he had everything he needed but more experience? Writing takes practice. Maybe that's what all those essays were for. Learning the typewriter the way a musician learns a saxophone. Once you do, you can play. Oh, he's a fool not to notice the obvious. Here's the kind of fool he was: He was sinking so far into an imaginary world, he missed half of what was happening around him. Finding happiness shouldn't have been so hard.

86. *computers*

Computers were just starting to invade the culture at this time. The library still had a card catalog, phones were attached to walls, students took notes on paper, Gypsum wrote everything on a typewriter, when the old lady at the dining hall was dealt a robotic blow. Who knows how long she had been standing guard at the doorway? She was like the lion on the steps of the art museum. She made sure students had a meal plan before letting them in. She had a binder full of names, but it didn't take her long to memorize everyone. That was her talent. She got a lot of happiness greeting you by name, waving you in. But one day a computer appeared in her spot. From then on students scanned their ID card. She was replaced by a red laser and a beep. The enlightened machinery of the 21st century was on the way.

87. *luck*

There was an L in her name. Was there a Y? Maybe a J…
It's hard to say. Sometimes she would ride in the hydroplane
with Jed and Gypsum, sitting in the backseat. She would listen
to them and laugh. Gypsum loved hearing that. She probably
liked him too and he liked her long brown hair and her smile,
but he never guessed what was going on. He saw her for the
last time outside the library in the summery dusk. The end was
happening fast, they were both graduating. He would never see
her again. When they said goodbye, he wished her good luck in
the days ahead. She would be fine—he was the one who would
need luck.

88. *advice*

Very few workers are left around here. Some of them are picketing outside. Some of them have read ahead and spread the word. Rumors abound. I don't want to know. I'd rather find out when I get there. If this continues though, I'll be the only one left. So what can I do? What advice can I give these last dejected interns and temps except…be understanding. You'll see, you're young, life can take hold of you too and take you to places you never dreamed. Not bad, right? This narrator is also available for commencement speeches.

89. *lifted*

One late morning, Gypsum went to Sacco's house. Queen Street was sunny and peaceful, everything gleamed, it was a perfect day to do something. Gypsum looked in the kitchen cupboard for coffee. There wasn't a lot to offer. Mother Hubbard would have felt at home. But he did find a bag full of beans—navy, pinto, black, kidney, lima, black-eyed peas—all mixed together like buckshot. The window showed sunshine on the green lawn spread across to the fraternity house. That's when it hit him. Gypsum tossed the weighty bag from hand to hand. "Come on!" he called Sacco, "Let's bean Beta House!" They ran out into the yard and took turns digging handfuls of beans. The sound rattled against the slats and rained down around the foundation. Then they ran back to the house, collapsing out of breath. They couldn't believe they didn't get caught. By nightfall the beans had taken root in the soil. Moonlight flowed, magic beanstalks lifted Beta up, white pillars and all.

90. *summertime*

There aren't any more workers here, just me. Someone sabotaged the fuse box. I hope the next book I do isn't this difficult. I'm typing this out by candlelight. The meter on the memory machine shows EMPTY. I'll try to make these last moments last. I have faith in the kid. I know I've been calling him a fool all along, but now I don't want him to end. What if everyone is wrong, what if his story is about to change course? It's my job to add the last couple chapters. What if I write it my own way? I already have an idea. That showbiz hypnotist returns to Magic Island. Summertime is near. He parks in the visitor lot and is crossing campus. He watches the students, remembers that performance at the gymnasium and he wonders if they ever found that chicken. He hopes so. Suddenly he bumps into Gypsum Tweed. In that moment of surprise, the hypnotist can tell a fellow traveler when he sees one. He tells Gypsum not to worry, this path goes on and on for as long as you.

91. *dandelions*

Gypsum made dandelions grow all over the lush green grass. It wasn't a difficult conjuring, not after four years at Magic Island. He sat on a rock and thought of bringing the flock all the way down to the beach. Dandelions don't like getting too close to the sea. That saltwater stings and they've heard stories of the strange plants underwater. Kelp and weeds. Barnacles and anemones. Whales bigger than a house. He got up and the dandelions followed along with him, down the steps to the shore. The flowers hissed and bumped into each other on the rocks, but they hurried to catch up with him, running on their roots across the sand, and before he walked into the shallows, they quickly floated under his feet to make a yellow raft.

92. *ending*

He said goodbye to everyone. Rooms were empty, echoing. People were disappearing. It didn't feel like he wouldn't be seeing them again. Cars were leaving, the way they arrived four years ago. Jim McBrady would be here soon. Gypsum could tell it was ending, there was no time to think of that. He went outside. Sun was shining, Magic Island sunk in the leaves, it was sending students out like bees. The trees on both sides of Belmont Street were full of birds. They sounded strange like they were singing backwards. The sky was melting the tops of the pines. The chapel tower looked like a candle. A puddle of sun gleamed on the quad.

Suddenly he thought of Agatha Mersey.

He started to run.

93. *time*

All of it was fading. Cupboard Hall was melting ever so slowly. Soon it would be the top floors of the dorms and old Hawthorne. Along with the trees, Magic Island was being erased. People were already vanishing. The lots were full of cars, packed to the gills, going home. Agatha's room was on a second floor, how much time was left? He had to hurry. He ran across campus, across Park Row and had to stop at Main Street. After a yellow pickup rattled by, he ran between the cars. He got to her house and clomped up the wooden steps of 238 Main, onto the porch and opened the door. It already felt like a memory. He leaped up the stairs two at a time.

94. *agatha*

Did he ever do anything romantic for Agatha Mersey? I'm not sure. Let's be honest, there's no tangible evidence. But there's one thing I learned about Gypsum Tweed—he was full of surprises. I would like to take credit for this, but believe it or not, he did it himself, without my help. I didn't notice that he picked a moonflower and brought it inside, up the stairs, past the picture on the wall. He turned and stopped outside her door. He knocked. He called her name through the door. He knew she stayed up late. She wouldn't go to sleep until after 2:22. Then, he turned the doorknob and looked. Across the room, he could see her lying in bed. She was wearing red and green flannel pajamas. She wasn't answering him. Her face was buried in the pillow. He carried the moonflower to her and set it on the table beside her. Next to the broken clock he gave her. He didn't want to wake her. If she really was asleep… How could she be? He was right beside her…talking to her…I don't know what she was thinking. Oh, if only someone was able to read her mind the way we've unraveled Gypsum Tweed. He knew when he went back downstairs and turned around, Agatha would be gone, replaced by the sky.

95. *memories*

When Gypsum Tweed left Magic Island, he lost the girl and everything else, people he knew and all the places he had been. He lost time in a way he never knew. Is that what Magic Island was teaching? All the homework, essays, tests and deadlines were dreary, but after this book is done you've seen what was wrapped around them. Were they trying to make him think of time a different way? He wouldn't know, he didn't take "Introduction to Time."

Somehow he wasn't quite there, maybe he felt us interfering, using this futuristic machine of ours, maybe we should have left him alone. No, it was worth it, wasn't it? Anyway, we've written another book.

The memory machine sighs. The last reel of film is flipping in its wheel.

Four years there had changed Gypsum Tweed. Magic Island worked slow magic on him, things that happened there did follow him. They gave him a shadow.

If he was a moth, he could have flown from it. Maybe that's what he did, he became a moth at the end, opened big rough woolen wings. Memories would be left for a time, long enough for some narrator to catch them out of the air. We don't know what happened next. Our last memory of him is walking on dandelions across the water.

96. *signing off*

Like a rocket radio signal fading into space, this is the narrator signing off. A little blue dot on the glass screen of the memory machine. Small as planet Earth in a telescope.

MAGIC ISLAND
Written during Fall 2021

Illustration from *Cosmonaut* (2021)

Books by Good Deed Rain

Saint Lemonade, Allen Frost, 2014. Two novels illustrated by the author in the manner of the old Big Little Books.

Playground, Allen Frost, 2014. Poems collected from seven years of chapbooks.

Roosevelt, Allen Frost, 2015. A Pacific Northwest novel set in July, 1942, when a boy and a girl search for a missing elephant. Illustrated throughout by Fred Sodt.

5 Novels, Allen Frost, 2015. Novels written over five years, featuring circus giants, clockwork animals, detectives and time travelers.

The Sylvan Moore Show, Allen Frost, 2015. A short story omnibus of 193 stories written over 30 years.

Town in a Cloud, Allen Frost, 2015. A three part book of poetry, written during the Bellingham rainy seasons of fall, winter, and spring.

A Flutter of Birds Passing Through Heaven: A Tribute to Robert Sund, 2016. Edited by Allen Frost and Paul Piper. The story of a legendary Ish River poet & artist.

At the Edge of America, Allen Frost, 2016. Two novels in one book blend time travel in a mythical poetic America.

Lake Erie Submarine, Allen Frost, 2016. A two week vacation in Ohio inspired these poems, illustrated by the author.

and Light, Paul Piper, 2016. Poetry written over three years. Illustrated with watercolors by Penny Piper.

The Book of Ticks, Allen Frost, 2017. A giant collection of 8 mysterious adventures featuring Phil Ticks. Illustrated throughout by Aaron Gunderson.

I Can Only Imagine, Allen Frost, 2017. Five adventures of love and heartbreak dreamed in an imaginary world. Cover & color illustrations by Annabelle Barrett.

The Orphanage of Abandoned Teenagers, Allen Frost, 2017. A fictional guide for teens and their parents. Illustrated by the author.

In the Valley of Mystic Light: An Oral History of the Skagit Valley Arts Scene, 2017. A comprehensive illustrated tribute. Edited by Claire Swedberg & Rita Hupy.

Different Planet, Allen Frost, 2017. Four science fiction adventures: reincarnation, robots, talking animals, outer space and clones. Cover & illustrations by Laura Vasyutynska.

Go with the Flow: A Tribute to Clyde Sanborn, 2018. Edited by Allen Frost. The life and art of a timeless river poet. In beautiful living color!

Homeless Sutra, Allen Frost, 2018. Four stories: Sylvan Moore, a flying monk, a water salesman, and a guardian rabbit.

The Lake Walker, Allen Frost 2018. A little novel set in black and white like one of those old European movies about death and life.

A Hundred Dreams Ago, Allen Frost, 2018. A winter book of poetry and prose. Illustrated by Aaron Gunderson.

Almost Animals, Allen Frost, 2018. A collection of linked stories, thinking about what makes us animals.

The Robotic Age, Allen Frost, 2018. A vaudeville magician and his faithful robot track down ghosts. Illustrated throughout by Aaron Gunderson.

Kennedy, Allen Frost, 2018. This sequel to *Roosevelt* is a coming-of-age fable set during two weeks in 1962 in a mythical Kennedyland. Illustrated throughout by Fred Sodt.

Fable, Allen Frost, 2018. There's something going on in this country and I can best relate it in fable: the parable of the rabbits, a bedtime story, and the diary of our trip to Ohio.

Elbows & Knees: Essays & Plays, Allen Frost, 2018. A thrilling collection of writing about some of my favorite subjects, from B-movies to Brautigan.

The Last Paper Stars, Allen Frost 2019. A trip back in time to the 20 year old mind of Frankenstein, and two other worlds of the future.

Walt Amherst is Awake, Allen Frost, 2019. The dreamlife of an office worker. Illustrated throughout by Aaron Gunderson.

When You Smile You Let in Light, Allen Frost, 2019. An atomic love story written by a 23 year old.

Pinocchio in America, Allen Frost, 2019. After 82 years buried underground, Pinocchio returns to life behind a car repair shop in America.

Taking Her Sides on Immortality, Robert Huff, 2019. The long awaited poetry collection from a local, nationally renowned master of words.

Florida, Allen Frost, 2019. Three days in Florida turned into a book of sunshine inspired stories.

Blue Anthem Wailing, Allen Frost, 2019. My first novel written in college is an apocalyptic, Old Testament race through American shadows while Amelia Earhart flies overhead.

The Welfare Office, Allen Frost, 2019. The animals go in and out of the office, leaving these stories as footprints.

Island Air, Allen Frost, 2019. A detective novel featuring haiku, a lost library book and streetsongs.

Imaginary Someone, Allen Frost, 2020. A fictional memoir featuring 45 years of inspirations and obstacles in the life of a writer.

Violet of the Silent Movies, Allen Frost, 2020. A collection of starry-eyed short story poems, illustrated by the author.

The Tin Can Telephone, Allen Frost, 2020. A childhood memory novel set in 1975 Seattle, illustrated by author like a coloring book.

Heaven Crayon, Allen Frost, 2020. How the author's first book *Ohio Trio* would look if printed as a Big Little Book. Illustrated by the author.

Old Salt, Allen Frost, 2020. Authors of a fake novel get chased by tigers. Illustrations by the author.

A Field of Cabbages, Allen Frost, 2020. The sequel to *The Robotic Age* finds our heroes in a race against time to save Sunny Jim's ghost. Illustrated by Aaron Gunderson.

River Road, Allen Frost, 2020. A paperboy delivers the news to a ghost town. Illustrated by the author.

The Puttering Marvel, Allen Frost, 2021. Eleven short stories with illustrations by the author.

Something Bright, Allen Frost, 2021. 106 short story poems walking with you from winter into spring. Illustrated by the author.

The Trillium Witch, Allen Frost, 2021. A detective novel about witches in the Pacific Northwest rain. Illustrated by the author.

Cosmonaut, Allen Frost, 2021. Yuri Gagarin stars in this novel that follows his rocket landing in an American town. Midnight jazz, folk music, mystery and sorcery. Illustrated by the author.

Thriftstore Madonna, Allen Frost, 2021. 124 summer story poems. Illustrated by the author.

Half a Giraffe, Allen Frost, 2021. A magical novel about a counterfeiter and his unusual, beloved pet. Illustrated by the author.

Lexington Brown & The Pond Projector, Allen Frost, 2022. An underwater invention takes three friends through time. Illustrated by Aaron Gunderson.

The Robert Huck Museum, Allen Frost, 2022. The artist's life story told in photographs, woodcuts, paintings, prints and drawings.

Mrs. Magnusson & Friends, Allen Frost, 2022. A collection of 13 stories featuring mystery and magic and ginkgo leaves.

Magic Island, Allen Frost, 2022. There's a memory machine in this magic novel that takes us to college.